Oliver's
Must-Do List

by
Susan Taylor Brown

Illustrated by Mary Sullivan

Boyds Mills Press

For Connor, and always for Erik
—S. T. B.

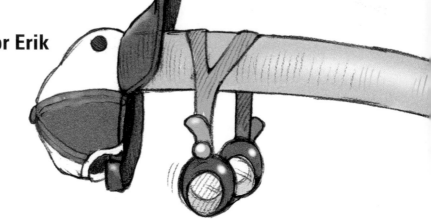

To mom and dad
—M. S.

Text copyright © 2005 by Susan Taylor Brown
Illustrations copyright © 2005 by Mary Sullivan

Published by Boyds Mills Press, Inc.
A Highlights Company
815 Church Street
Honesdale, Pennsylvania 18431
Printed in China
Visit our Web site at www.boydsmillspress.com

Library of Congress Cataloging-in-Publication Data

Brown, Susan Taylor, 1958-
  Oliver's must-do list / by Susan Taylor Brown ; illustrated by Mary Sullivan.
      p. cm.
Summary: Together Oliver and his mother play through their "to do" list.
ISBN 1-59078-198-8 (alk. paper)
[1. Play—Fiction. 2. Parent and child—Fiction.] I. Sullivan, Mary, 1958- ill. II. Title.

PZ7.B8179Ol 2005
[E]—dc22   *34890466 3/07*
    2004029086CIP

First edition, 2005
The text of this book is set in 15-point Clearface Regular.
The illustrations are done digitally.

10 9 8 7 6 5 4 3 2 1

In the morning, Oliver asked his mother, "Will you play with me today?"

"Let me check today's Must-Do list."

Oliver's mother had a list of all the things she needed to do. She kept the list on the refrigerator. Some days it was a very long list. She gave Oliver a hug.

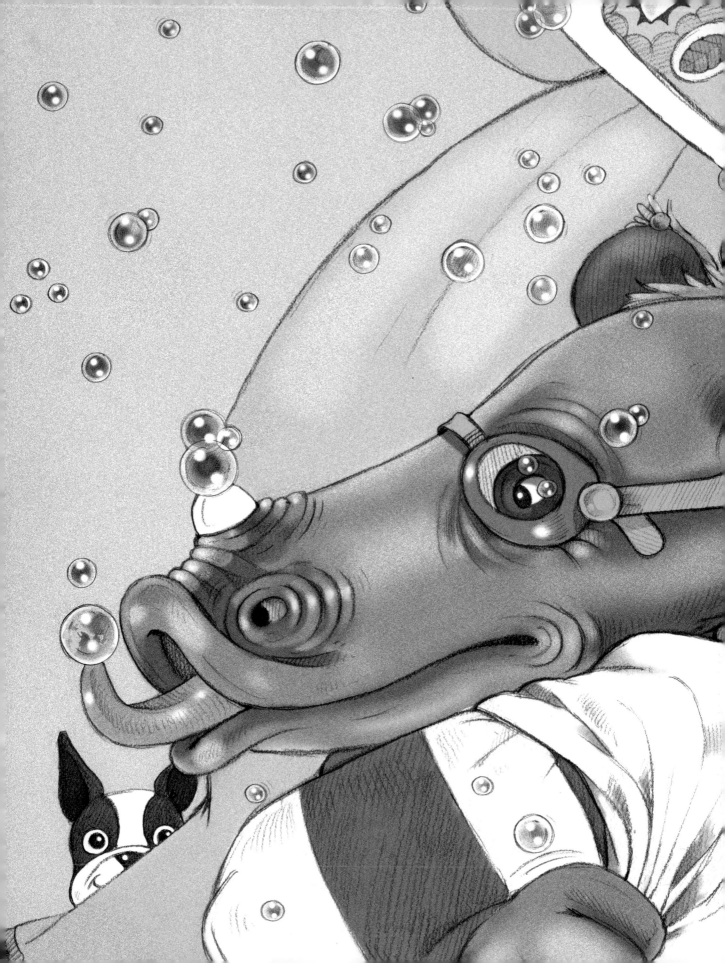

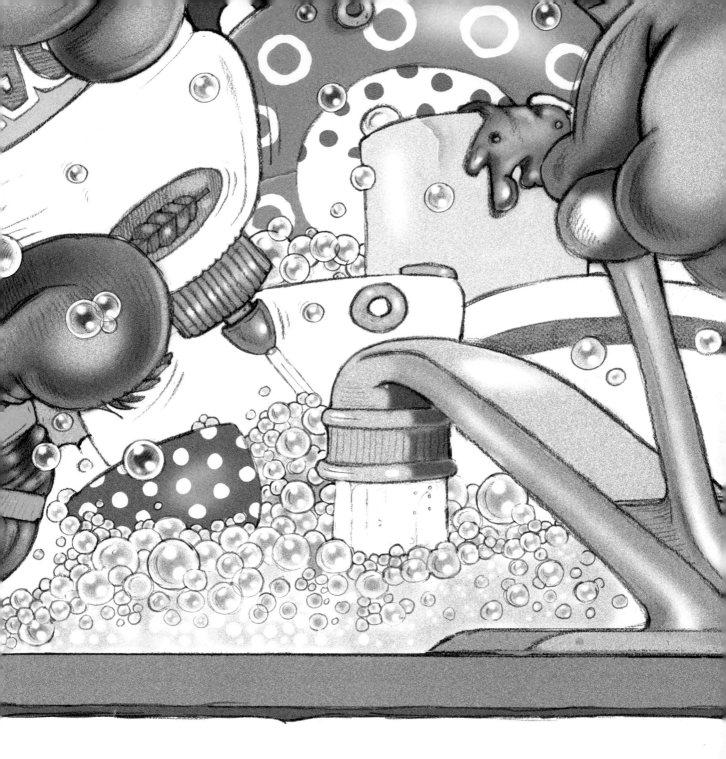

"Oh, Oliver, I wish I could play, but not now. First I have to wash the breakfast dishes. Then it will be time to do the laundry."

She squirted dish soap into the sink, and little bubbles floated into the air.

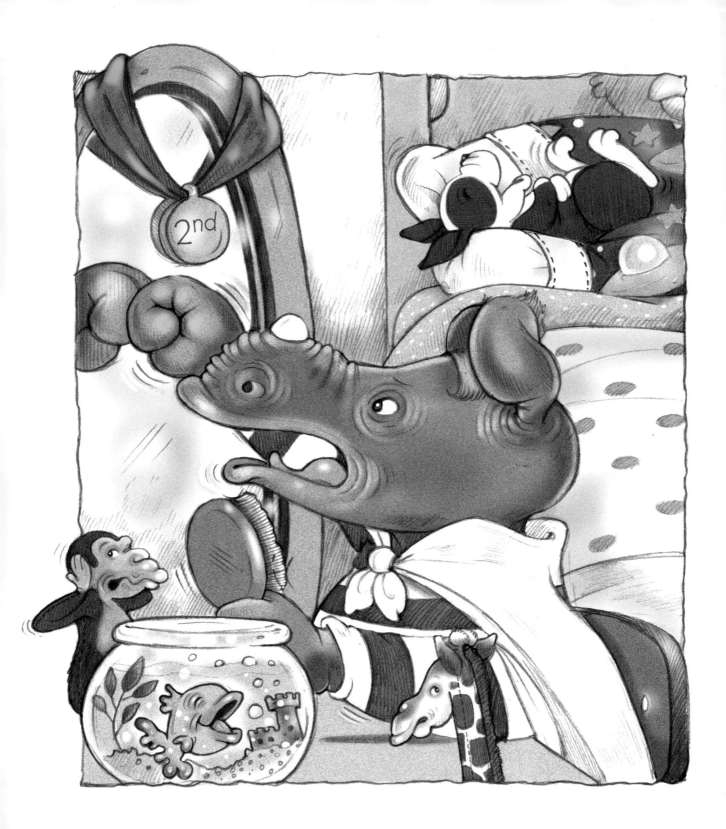

Oliver practiced his knock-knock jokes in front of his bedroom mirror, but it wasn't the same without someone to say, "Who's there?"

He took a kitchen chair and laid it on the floor. He pretended it was a racecar and zoomed around the room, but it wasn't much fun without someone to race against.

Oliver watched his mother fold the laundry. He grabbed his favorite red shirt and held it up to his nose to smell the clean.

"Will you play with me now?" he asked.

Oliver's mother checked her Must-Do list, then blew him a kiss. "Oh, Oliver, I wish I could play, but not now. I have to do the ironing. Then it will be time to go to the grocery store."

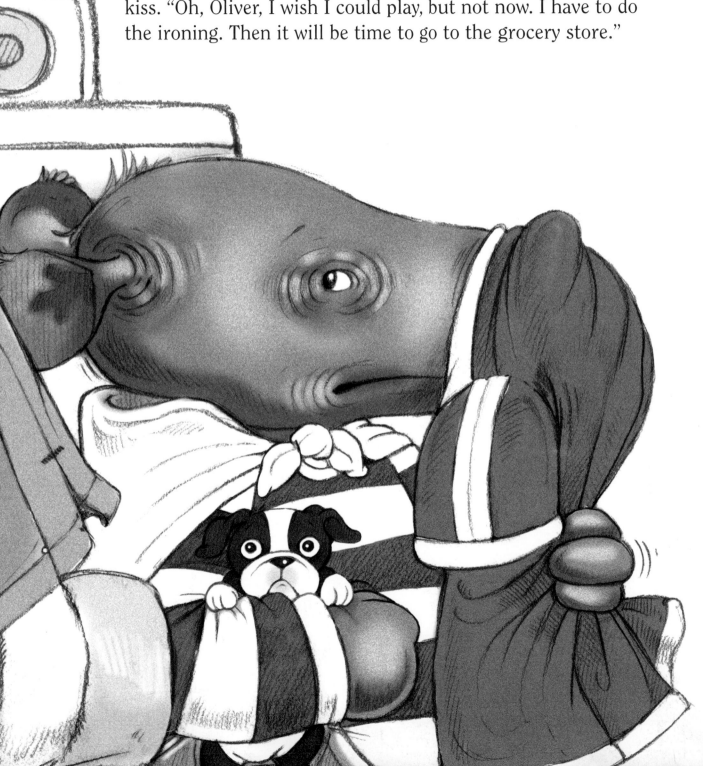

Oliver pulled all the cushions off the couch and tried to build a fort, but the walls kept falling down.

"It's no fun having an adventure without someone to share it with," he said.

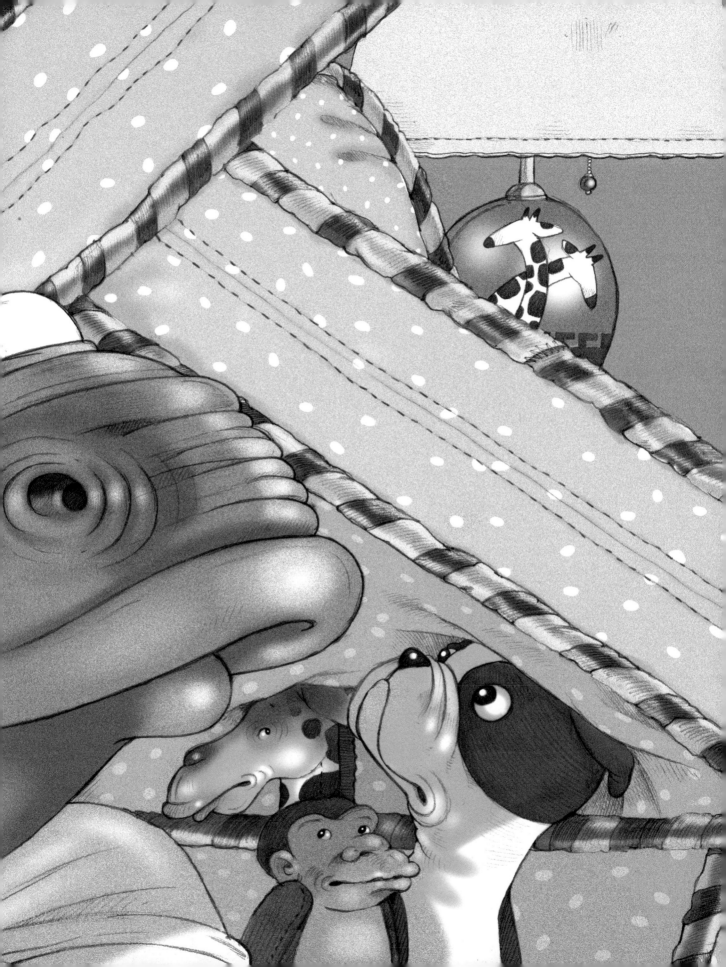

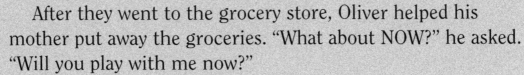

After they went to the grocery store, Oliver helped his
mother put away the groceries. "What about NOW?" he asked.
"Will you play with me now?"

"Goodness, no! Why just look at this list. So much work
still to do. Clean the bathroom. Vacuum. Dust. Mop the floors.
Then it will be time for dinner."

Later, Oliver put on his pajamas and brushed his teeth. His mother came in to say good-night.

"What about now?" he whispered.

Oliver's mother yawned. "Oh, Oliver, I'm sorry. Maybe tomorrow." She tucked him into bed and turned out the light.

After she left, Oliver got out of bed and stared out the window. He tried to count the stars and find the Big Dipper, but he wasn't sure where to look.

The next morning, Oliver got up very early. He made his own Must-Do list and put it on the refrigerator. He made sure that his list covered his mother's list completely. He waited for his mother to come into the kitchen.

Oliver's mother read the list:

Tell a joke.

Drive a racecar.

Build a fort.

Count the stars and find the Big Dipper.

She sighed. She put her hands on her hips and started to whistle. She tapped her foot. Oliver waited. And waited and waited and waited . . .

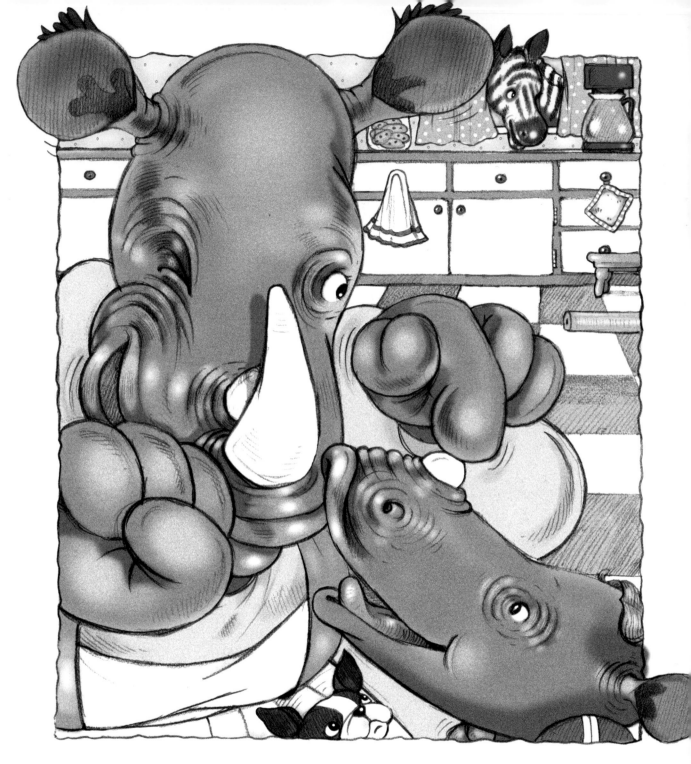

"Knock, knock," she said.
"Who's there?" said Oliver.
"Wooden shoe."
"Wooden shoe who?"
"Wooden shoe like to play with me today?"

Oliver laughed. "You told a joke."

Oliver's mother winked at him. "Well, it IS on the list."

"I don't suppose," said Oliver, "that you know how to drive a racecar, do you?"

"Not only that, I know the perfect racetrack," she said. "Follow me."

Oliver's mother grabbed the pillows off the bed and showed Oliver how to race down the stairs on his stomach over and over again until they collapsed in a heap at the bottom of the stairs.

Oliver won almost every time.

She tickled him, and they both giggled so hard that they got the hiccups.

"Do you know how to build a fort?" asked Oliver.
"I'll have you know I am a champion fort builder."
Oliver's mother pulled out the card table and draped a big blanket over the top.

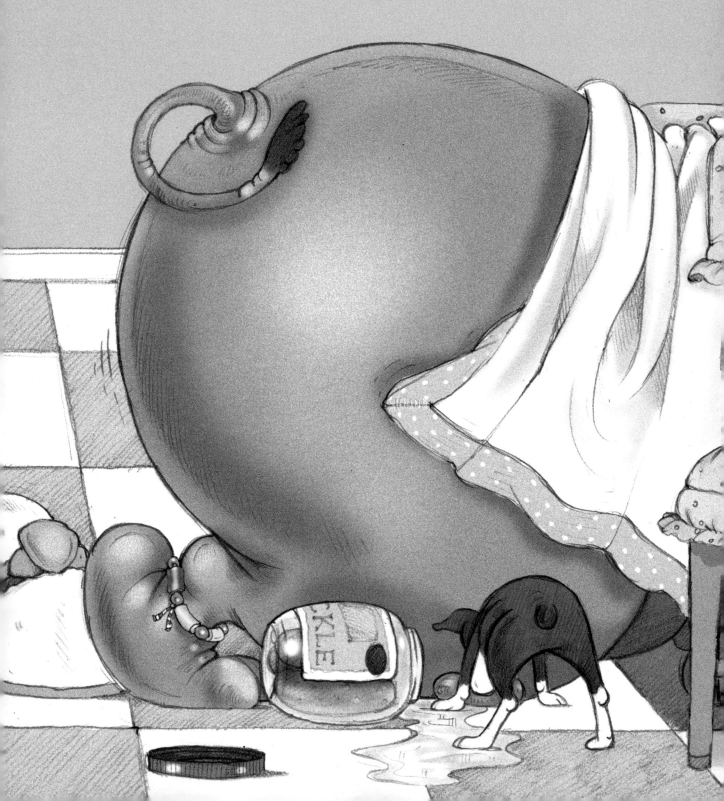

She took all the kitchen chairs and made a big wall around the fort. Inside the fort they ate peanut-butter-and-pickle sandwiches and played cards and sang silly songs.

"Shush," she said. "Do you hear that? I think pirates are trying to attack the fort."

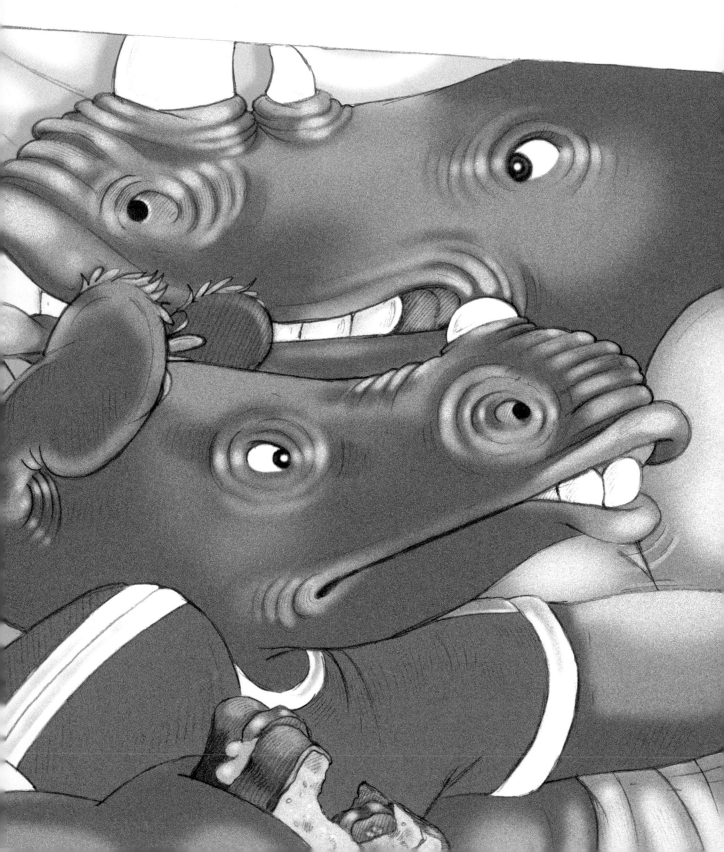

Oliver grabbed his imaginary sword. "I'll save you!" he shouted.
"Take that and that!" yelled Oliver's mother.
Together they battled pirates.

"They got me," cried Oliver. He stumbled out of the fort, clutching his hand to his chest. He spun around in a circle three times and collapsed onto the floor.

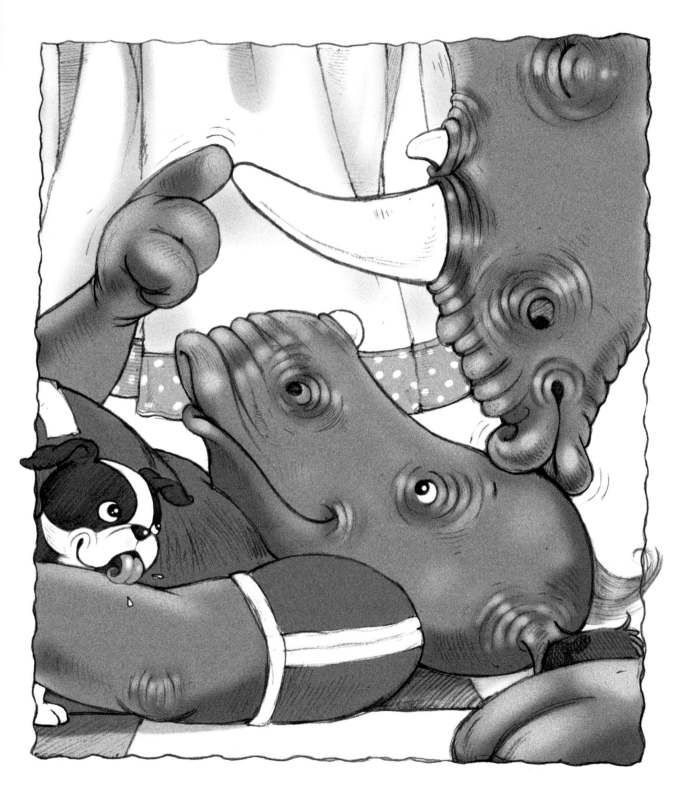

Oliver's mother kissed him on the forehead. "My hero," she said.

After dinner, Oliver had a bath and put on his pajamas. "I guess it's time for bed?"

"Not yet," said his mother. "There's still one thing left on our list."

She took some pillows and a big quilt outside to their backyard. Together they counted the stars and listened to the crickets sing. They even found the Big Dipper.

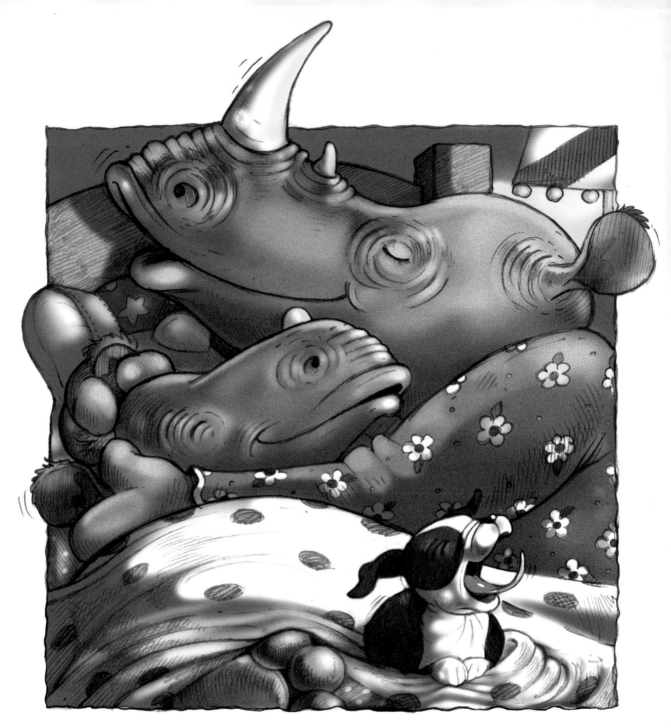

"Knock, knock," said Oliver.

"Who's there?"

"Hank."

"Hank who?"

"Hank you for playing with me today."

Oliver's mother smiled and snuggled close.

"Hank you — for making such a good list."